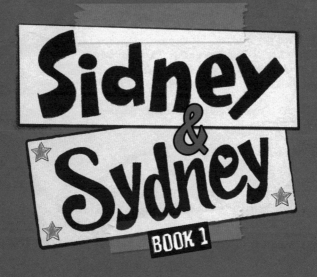

Third Grade Mix-Up

by Michele Jakubowski ★ illustrated by Luisa Montalto

PICTURE WINDOW BOOKS
a capstone imprint

Sidney & Sydney is published by Picture Window Books
A Capstone Imprint
1710 Roe Crest Drive
North Mankato, Minnesota 56003
www.capstonepub.com

Library of Congress Cataloging-in-Publication Data is available on the
Library of Congress website.

ISBN: 978-1-4048-8001-6 (hardcover)
ISBN: 978-1-4048-8104-4 (paper over board)

Summary: When Sidney Fletcher moves to Oak Grove, things get a little
strange for Sydney Greene. Not only does Sydney share a name with a
boy, but he's in her third-grade class! From first-day-of-school problems
to Halloween drama, Sidney and Sydney quickly become friends. Who
says boys and girls can't get along?

Design by Kay Fraser

Printed in China.
092012
006936RRDS13

FOR JACK AND MIA. ALL MY LOVE.
—M.J.

TABLE OF CONTENTS

Name: Sydney Shelby Baxter Greene

Age: 8

Birthdate: August 3

Parents: Bob and Jane Greene

Siblings: Owen, a charming and annoying baby brothe

Hobbies: fashion, playing *Galaxy Conquest*, reading

Sydney and best friend Harley

Sydney Greene

is a sassy third grader. Not onl does she love fashion, but she loves a good game of *Galaxy Conquest* as well. She might b the smallest kid in the class, but she's also the spunkiest! Her best friend is Harley Livingston, a third-grade soccer star. They have been best friends since preschool, when Harley kicked a soccer ball into Sydney's face.

Name: Sidney Patrick Fletcher

Age: 8

Birthdate: May 11

Parents: Paula Fletcher

Siblings: None

Hobbies: sports, playing *Galaxy Conquest*, telling jokes

Sidney and best friend Gomez

Sidney Fletcher

is a quiet kid who loves sports. He is also the newest third grader in Oak Grove. However, it doesn't take him long to make friends. Gomez (whose real name is Marco Xavier Gomez) is Sidney's first and best friend in Oak Grove. With one joke at the bus stop, Sidney and Gomez become inseparable.

CHAPTER 1

Can't Hide from School

"Sidney! Wake up or you're going to be late for the first day at your new school!"

I heard my mom yelling to me. I don't know why she yells. It doesn't make me want to get up any faster. All I wanted to do was stay in bed. I didn't want to go to that stupid new school anyway.

But moms never give up. She came in my room and pulled off my blanket. I tried to hide under my pillow, but it was too small.

"Come on, Sid. You're going to be late," Mom said.

"I don't want to go," I grumbled from under my pillow.

"It will be fun," Mom said. "You're going to the same school I went to when I was your age!"

Mom had been telling me that ever since we moved to Oak Grove. She grew up here. And for some reason, she thought it was so great that I'd be going to her old school.

I didn't see how it made things any better to be going to the same school she went to a million years ago. It made me think that the building must be really old. It could probably fall down at any moment.

I was happy we had moved to Oak Grove. When my mom and I lived in Chicago, it got sort of lonely. It was a huge city, but it was just the two of us since my dad died.

I liked living in the city, but now we had a huge backyard. Plus, in Oak Grove we only lived a block and six houses from Granny and Grandpa.

What I wasn't happy about was going to a new school. What if all the kids were mean? What if I didn't like it?

"I guess I'll have to eat that big bowl of Fruity Frosted Loopies," my mom said.

I poked my head out from under the pillow.

"You got my favorite cereal?" I asked.

"Yep, just for you," she said.

I jumped out of bed. I still wasn't
excited about going to a new school, but
it wasn't every day my mom got me Fruity
Frosted Loopies!

CHAPTER 2

Fruity Frosted Loopies Can't Fix Everything

Today was a big day. Today I finally got to wear the new outfit I had picked out weeks ago. And as I got ready for the first day of third grade, I knew I had made the right choice.

I checked over my outfit. Cute tunic? Check. Cute leggings? Check. Cute headband? Check. And the best part of all: purple ankle boots.

You may not think a first day of school outfit is important, but I do. I'm only eight years old, but it's never too early to be fashionable.

I am the first person to notice when my mom's shoes don't match her outfit. She doesn't mind. She says I have "an eye for fashion," whatever that means. Sometimes my parents say the weirdest things!

"Sydney!" I heard my mom call. "Hurry up or you'll miss the bus."

I walked slowly down the stairs and into the kitchen. I had a big frown on my face. You would think that with such a cute first-day-of-school outfit I would be happy about going back to school, but I wasn't.

"Cheer up," my mom said. "You're going to love third grade!"

That's what I thought until five days ago. That's when we found out our classroom

assignments. Ever since preschool I have been in the same class as my best friend, Harley Livingston. But not this year.

Harley got Mrs. Madden, who is super nice and smells like cherries. I got Mr. Luther. He is grumpy and doesn't smell like anything.

"Buck up, kiddo!" my dad said as he fed my baby brother, Owen, a spoonful of cereal.

I frowned bigger because I don't even know what "buck up" means. See what I mean about my parents and the weird things they say?

Owen must have thought it was weird too. He stuck out his tongue and sprayed cereal all over my dad's shirt.

Even though I didn't want to, I laughed.

I smiled a little bigger when Mom pulled out Fruity Frosted Loopies, which is my favorite cereal. She doesn't let me eat sugar cereal very often, but today was special. How could I stay mad with this delicious cereal in front of me?

"Eat up," Mom said as she put my lunch bag into my new backpack.

Then I quickly remembered where I was going and went right back to my bad mood.

Not even sugar cereal could keep me happy today.

CHAPTER 3

The Bus Stop and Gomez Gomez

At the bus stop, there was a short kid kicking a hole in the ground with his shoe.

"Gomez, stop digging up the Petersons' yard!" the woman standing near him said. The kid looked up at her. Then he moved to another spot and began a new hole.

"Good morning!" the woman said when she saw us. "You must be the people who bought the Garcias' old house. It's so nice to meet you! I'm Florence Gomez, and this is my son, Gomez."

My eyes bugged out of my head. Had she just said her last name was Gomez?

And her son's name was Gomez? So his name was Gomez Gomez! How cool was that?

Gomez's mom must have been reading my mind. The next thing I heard her say was, "His first name is Marco, but everyone has called him Gomez since he was a baby."

My mom and Mrs. Gomez kept talking, the way moms always do. I looked over at Gomez. He was still hard at work on his hole. I am tall for my age, and he was a lot shorter than me.

"Say hello to Gomez, Sidney," my mom said. "Mrs. Gomez says you two will be in the same class. Isn't that nice?"

I put on one of those fake smiles I do sometimes. I pull my lips wide across my face, and only I know that I'm not really smiling.

Gomez looked up at me and began to laugh a little bit. I wanted to see if I could really crack him up so I crossed my eyes and stuck out my tongue. He started laughing so hard I thought the kid was going to pee his pants!

It was at that moment that I knew Gomez and I were going to be best friends. Maybe school wouldn't be so bad after all.

CHAPTER 4

Sydney with a "y" Meets Sidney with an "i"

I had never walked into a classroom without Harley next to me. I was so nervous!

Mr. Luther was standing in the middle of the room saying hello to everyone. I looked around to see if there was anyone I knew.

I saw Gomez and Alexa, who both lived on my block. I also saw Nick, James, and Rebecca, who were in my class last year. Nick was a bully, but the other kids were nice.

Then Mr. Luther said, "Everyone, find your seats! Your place at the table will have your name on it."

I was happy when I found my seat right away. I noticed that Mr. Luther had spelled my name wrong. He had spelled it Sidney, instead of Sydney. Mr. Luther was busy helping some other kids find their seats, so I decided to tell him later.

"Hey, Squidney!" Nick said as he sat down across from me. He had been calling me that since kindergarten.

My mom and dad told me to ignore people when they say mean things, so that's what I did.

Before Nick could say anything else, I saw Mr. Luther walking across the room with a new kid. Mr. Luther looked confused as he got to my table.

"I thought I had put you over here," he was saying to the boy. He looked at my name tag and smiled at me. "You must be Sydney."

Mr. Luther may not have smelled like cherries, but he did have a nice smile.

"Yes, I am," I said.

"Well, Sydney, let me introduce you to Sidney," Mr. Luther said, pointing to the new boy.

"Uh, okay, hi," I said.

The new boy was very tall and had black hair that fell over his eyes. He was looking at the ground when he mumbled, "Hi."

"I think you may be sitting in the wrong spot, Sydney," Mr. Luther told me, pointing to the name tag. "See? This Sidney spells his name with an 'I.'"

I felt my cheeks start to burn. How embarrassing! By now all of the other kids had found their seats. Everyone was staring at me!

"Here's your seat, Sydney with a 'Y'!" I heard James call from across the room.

I stood up slowly and began to walk across the room. This was just too embarrassing! As I passed Nick he said, "Way to go, Squidney with a 'Y'. By third grade you should know how to spell your own name!"

This was turning into the worst first day of school ever!

CHAPTER 5

The Scariest Place on Earth Is the Cafeteria

Besides having my seat stolen by
that little blond girl, my morning had
gone fine. During the first recess I played
basketball with Gomez. I was feeling
pretty good until it was time to go in
for lunch. The playground lady called
for Mr. Luther's class to line up.

"Come on, Gomez, let's go eat," I said.
I was really hungry, and my mom is an
excellent lunch packer.

"I can't," Gomez said. "I have to go to
the nurse's office."

"Are you sick?" I asked.

"No," he said.

"So why are you going to the nurse's office?" I asked.

"I'm diabetic, so I need to get my blood sugar checked before lunch," Gomez said. "My mom worries. She wants me to eat lunch with the nurse for the first few days of school, just to be on the safe side."

I must have had a strange look on my face, because then Gomez said, "Don't worry, you can't catch diabetes!"

I have to admit that I was relieved, but I was still confused.

"What is diabetes?" I asked.

"My body has trouble making insulin, which it needs to get energy. I get my blood sugar checked and insulin shots to help it," Gomez explained.

"Shots?" I repeated, my eyes getting bigger. "Like the kind you get at the doctor that your parents say won't hurt but they really do?"

"Yep," Gomez said, nodding. "You get used to it. I'm pretty tough."

"I might be bigger, but you are definitely way tougher," I said.

Gomez looked very proud of himself. "Well, I'd better go. Miss Mary is actually pretty fun to eat with. She knows a lot of good jokes. See you later!"

After Gomez ran off, I walked slowly to the lunch line. When our class got into the cafeteria, everyone was sitting in groups talking loudly and eating their lunches. Everyone was smiling, laughing, and having fun. Everyone but me. I was terrified.

The cafeteria in a new school is the scariest place on Earth. In a new classroom, you are assigned a seat. In the cafeteria, you have to find one. And it is not an easy task.

I was too afraid to ask anyone if I could sit with them. I felt like my shoes had been glued to the floor. This was not going to end well for me.

Finally a cafeteria lady came over and put her arm around my shoulder. "Are you looking for a spot, sweetie?" she asked.

I just nodded. I felt like every eye in the cafeteria was on me. My face started to get very hot. Thankfully the nice woman guided me to an open table. There was a big sign in the middle that read Nut-Free Table. I guess that's where the kids who have nut allergies sit.

Even though I didn't have a nut allergy, I was more than happy to sit down. There were two kids sitting at the table already. They looked up and gave me annoyed looks. Then they went back to ignoring me. So much for feeling welcome!

I lowered my head and opened my lunch. A note from my mom fell onto the table.

I know that it's really dorky to get a note from your mom when you're eight years old. But it did make me feel a little better.

Hello, Sidney!

I hope you are having the best first day of third grade ever!

I love you!

Mom

CHAPTER 6

Weirder Things Have Happened

The doorbell was ringing, and my mom had just told me the craziest thing ever.

"You what?" I asked.

"I met the new neighbors today," she repeated. "I invited them for dinner. Mrs. Fletcher is great, and her son Sidney is in your class. Isn't that nice?"

After the name mix-up, the rest of my day had been pretty good. Now my mom was ruining it. Why would I want to hang out with the new boy? The same boy who had totally embarrassed me at school? Ugh.

I didn't have time to argue because the doorbell rang again and my mom opened the door. The new boy and his mom were here.

"Thank you so much for having us over," Mrs. Fletcher said.

"We're so glad you could come," my mom said and gave Mrs. Fletcher a hug. They had only met today, but the two of them acted like best friends. I guess that's what happens when you're old.

After introducing the guests to my dad, my mom turned toward me and said, "Why don't you take Sidney down to the basement before dinner?"

"Okay," I mumbled.

Sidney was standing with his hands in his pockets, looking at the floor. I've looked at our floor before. It's not that interesting.

He followed me down the stairs. I showed him my corner of the basement. My parents call it my "art studio." That makes me feel like a real artist.

Sidney walked around looking at all of the cool stuff on the walls. He stopped in front of a poster my aunt gave me of the Eiffel Tower in Paris.

"I'm going to go there someday," I told him. "I'm going to be a famous artist, a rock star, or a veterinarian when I grow up. I'm going to travel around the world. It's going to be amazing!"

"I've been to Paris. It's pretty cool," he said and shrugged.

I couldn't believe my ears! He said it like it was no big deal! As if he'd said, "I've been to the mall."

"Oh, I'm so jealous!" I told him. "Paris is the fashion capital of the world! The farthest I've ever been is to my grandparents' house in Florida."

He laughed and said, "My dad was a photographer. He used to take my mom and me with him when he worked."

"Where else have you been?" I asked.

"I've been all over the world," Sidney told me. "Besides France, I've been to Spain, China, and Australia."

"No way!" I said. I couldn't believe it.

He shrugged again and said, "It was cool. They took me to a lot of museums and historical places."

"I love museums! Especially art museums," I said.

"Me too!" he said. He seemed happy that I agreed. "Those were always my favorite. My mom is an artist, so we'd spend a lot of time looking at cool stuff. She knows all about it."

"Wow. Just wow," I said.

"Hey! Is that *Galaxy Conquest*?" he asked, walking over to the shelves where I kept my video games.

"Yes," I said quietly. None of my girl friends liked to play that game, but I loved playing it with my dad.

"That's my favorite video game ever!" he said. "I totally rule at *Galaxy Conquest*! Wanna play?"

I really did want to play, even if it was with a boy I barely knew. I couldn't help but think the following things as we set up the game: *Am I actually getting along with the new kid? A new kid who is a boy? The same new kid who shares my name and embarrassed me today? Weird!*

But I guess weirder things have happened.

CHAPTER 7

A Girl Friend, Not a Girlfriend

By the time Mrs. Greene called us up for dinner, Sydney and I had each won one game of *Galaxy Conquest*. We decided we'd play the championship round after dinner.

I hadn't been happy about going over to the Greenes' house when my mom first told me about the invitation. But Sydney was kind of cool. Plus, she really was good at *Galaxy Conquest*. And dinner was awesome!

As I finished up my second piece of lasagna, baby Owen began banging his hands on his high chair. I hadn't spent much time around babies, and the angry look on his face made me laugh. I looked over at Sydney and she was laughing too.

Owen must have noticed that he was making us laugh. He did it again. This time he banged so hard, a bunch of lasagna flew in the air. One got stuck in his hair. Another was just above his eye. He looked at us to see if we were still laughing. We were. I had no idea babies could be so funny!

After the meal, Mrs. Greene pulled fresh cookies out of the oven. Amazing! I was happily eating my second cookie when Sydney kicked me under the table. I looked up and saw her pointing at her brother. She said very quietly, "Watch this!"

Owen was munching on his cookie when he noticed that we were looking at him again. Without her parents noticing, Sydney stuck out her tongue a few times very quickly. Owen laughed.

Then he began sticking out his tongue and slobbering all over. Soon enough, the mashed-up cookie in his mouth began flying all over the place! Mr. and Mrs. Greene were sitting on either side of Owen. In a flash, they were both covered in cookie slime.

At that same moment, I took a big gulp of milk. But Owen was laughing super hard. That made me laugh too. Have you ever tried to laugh when your mouth is full of milk? It doesn't work very well.

Next thing I knew, milk was spurting out of my nose! I looked at Sydney and she was laughing so hard she fell off her chair. Seeing that made me laugh even harder. Out came the last bit of milk.

What's going on here? I thought. *Am I actually getting along with a girl? Weird! But I guess weirder things have happened.*

Besides, a friend who is a girl is NOT a girlfriend.

CHAPTER 8

Day Two Isn't as Bad as Day One

Day two of third grade started out tough. When I got to my locker, Nick was waiting for me.

"Have you learned how to spell your name yet, Squidney with a 'Y'?" he asked meanly.

I tried to ignore him, but he just kept talking. But before I could get too mad, Sidney showed up.

"Oh, look. It's the other Sidney," Nick said. "The one who can spell his name. I guess you must be the smart one."

"Very funny," Sidney said.

"I know," Nick said. "I'm a pretty funny guy."

"I was being sarcastic," Sidney said.

"I knew that," Nick stuttered.

"Clearly," I said with a smile. As Nick was leaving, I made sure to call out, "If you make fun of our names again, there will be trouble!"

I may not have been as tall as Sidney, but I was no wimp. By lunchtime my day was going great. Harley and I had just sat down when I saw Sidney enter the cafeteria. He stood in the doorway for a moment, looking for a place to sit.

"Hey, Sidney!" I called out. "Want to sit with us?"

"Thanks," he said quietly as he sat down next to me.

"Sidney, this is my best friend, Harley," I said. "Harley, this is Sidney, but he spells his name with an 'I'."

"Gomez told me all about you," Harley said. "He said you're hilarious."

"Well, he would be correct," Sidney said as he smiled and opened his lunch.

"I forgot my milk. Be right back!" Harley said.

"You know, I thought you were weird when I first met you," I told Sidney.

Then I blushed. That wasn't at all how I meant to say it. The words just came out that way.

"I mean, you just stared at the ground and didn't say anything," I said.

Sidney seemed to understand, because right away he said, "I wasn't so sure about you, either. I don't usually have friends who are girls." He took a sip of milk and added, "But you're a pretty good *Galaxy Conquest* player."

"And you're pretty funny," I said.

Sidney laughed.

Before I could stop myself, I said, "So we're friends now?"

Sidney put down his milk. He looked up at me and smiled. "Yeah, I guess we are," he said.

I smiled and went back to eating my lunch. Maybe this year was going to be all right after all. But it was only day two of an entire year, so I wasn't going to get too excited yet.

CHAPTER 9

Halloween, Gomez, and One Mean Older Brother

After the first few weeks of school, I felt right at home. Gomez was the best friend I could ask for. Without him, school would be pretty lame. We spent a lot of time at his house. Gomez has three brothers and a sister, so there's always something going on. I'm an only child, so I love the noise.

And even though Sydney is a girl, we spent a lot of time together as well. Our moms were best friends, so it was pretty convenient. Plus our *Galaxy Conquest* games were really heating up.

Between hanging out with Gomez and Sydney (and Sydney's best friend Harley) and playing football, I was a happy kid. And before I knew it, it was the end of October and Halloween was just a few days away.

I guess Halloween is a big deal in Oak Grove. Gomez's family goes all out for Halloween. They set up an entire graveyard. It has about twenty tombstones. The tombstones have funny sayings on them like "I told you I was sick" and "Here lies good old Fred, a great big rock fell on his head."

I was helping Gomez set up Halloween decorations in his yard. He looked a little down.

"What's wrong, Gomez?" I asked.

Gomez didn't say anything. He just shrugged his shoulders and kept putting up the tombstones.

"Aren't you excited for Halloween?" I asked.

"Not really," he replied quietly.

"What? That's crazy!" I said. "I can't wait to go trick-or-treating! I bet I can get at least 100 pieces of candy. There are so many houses in our neighborhood!"

Gomez looked sad. "Yeah," he said glumly. "I bet you can."

"Seriously, what's wrong with you?" I asked him. I didn't want to be mean, but what was his problem? How could talking about candy make anybody sad?

Then I remembered that Gomez had diabetes and couldn't eat much sugar.

"Oh, right. You can't even eat the candy. Sorry, Gomez," I said.

Gomez shrugged. "I can have some candy, just not a lot," he said. "It's hard to collect all that candy and not eat it. That's one reason why I don't really like Halloween."

I was trying to think of a way to cheer him up when a giant monster jumped out of the bushes. Gomez and I both screamed!

My heart was still pounding when we realized that it wasn't a monster. It was Gomez's older brother, Lucas.

Lucas laughed and pointed at us as he took off his monster mask. "You should have seen the looks on your faces! What babies! I can't believe I scared you with this wimpy mask. "

Lucas was thirteen and always picking on Gomez. Gomez was used to it since he has such a big family. I don't have any brothers or sisters, so I thought it was mean.

"Boo!" Lucas shouted, making us both jump again. He laughed and began to walk away saying, "I just love Halloween."

Gomez frowned and muttered, "And that's one more reason I don't like Halloween."

CHAPTER 10

A Purple Superhero Princess

Every year my mom takes me shopping for a Halloween costume. I like dressing up, so I spend a long time picking out the right costume. That is why I get so mad when I see a bunch of kids wearing the same costume as me. Last year I was a cowgirl, and there were four other cowgirls in our school!

This year, things were going to be different. When Grandma Betty came for a visit this past summer, she offered to make me a Halloween costume.

How cool is that? I would have a completely original costume. What a dream!

I had the perfect costume in mind. I knew nobody else would think of it. I wanted to be a purple superhero princess. I sent Grandma Betty about a million drawings of exactly how I wanted it to look. I even mailed her a purple crayon to show her the exact color.

Now Halloween was only a week away, and my costume had arrived. And the dress was just perfect!

"Ta-da!" I shouted as I ran into my room. I twirled and jumped and twirled some more.

Harley was sitting on my bed waiting for me. She clapped her hands and cheered. "Oh, Sydney, it's beautiful!"

I twirled around a few times so she could get a good look at me. It was so fun. I wanted to keep twirling all day!

I know a lot of girls dress like princesses on Halloween, but they won't look like me. From the tiara on my head to the boots on my feet, my whole costume is purple. Plus, I have a cape. That's why it's a superhero princess costume, not just a regular princess costume. It's awesome!

This year I was going to win the prize for best costume for sure!

I started getting dizzy, so I stopped twirling. When I looked at Harley, she looked sad.

"What's wrong, Harley? Don't you like my costume?" I asked.

"Your costume is great," she said. "I just wish I was as excited about Halloween as you are."

When Harley was sad, I was sad. I plopped down next to her on my bed.

"But you've got a great costume! Why aren't you excited?" I asked.

Harley's older brother Leo was a football player at Oak Grove High School. He was letting her borrow his jersey from last year. Her parents got her some real football pads and everything. She was even going to draw black lines under her eyes like the football players on TV.

"It's not the costume, it's about trick-or-treating," Harley explained. "My mom has been on a health kick lately. She won't let me eat sugar. No gummy worms, candy bars, or taffy for me."

"Not even on a special holiday like Halloween?" I asked.

"Nope. My mom is pretty strict about her sugar rules," Harley replied.

I gave Harley a big hug. I wanted this to be the best Halloween ever, so I had to find a way to help Harley. After all, I was a purple superhero princess!

CHAPTER 11

One Problem at a Time

In case you don't remember, *Galaxy Conquest* is by far my favorite game of all time. I like any game where you have awesome powers and get to battle aliens. And I used to think I was the best player. Until I met Sydney.

Once we started playing together, we kept track of all of our games. So far she had won 52, and I'd won 48.

Two days before Halloween, we were playing our 101st game of *Galaxy Conquest* in Sydney's basement. Sydney was playing a good game and attacking me with her GX5000 laser. But I had a powerful force field, so she was in trouble.

"I win!" I shouted.

"Good game, Sidney," she muttered. She updated my score to 49. Neither of us liked losing (who does?), so I decided to talk about something else.

"Can you believe Halloween is on Friday?" I asked. "I can't wait to go trick-or-treating!"

That made Sydney smile. "And I can't wait to see who wins best costume at school!" she said.

Sydney had been keeping her costume a surprise. From the way she acted, I knew it must be something good. It was probably a super girly costume, but I'm sure it was still pretty cool.

My mom had taken me to the Halloween store. I got a cool magician costume. It had a cape and a real magician hat that folded down and then popped back up. My grandpa had been teaching me card tricks too.

I noticed that the look on Sydney's face had changed. She looked sad again.

"What's wrong?" I asked.

"I was just thinking about Harley," she said. "She doesn't really like Halloween.

Her mom is on a health kick and won't let her eat any of the candy."

"Even on a special holiday like Halloween?" I asked.

"Nope. I said the same thing! It's crazy," Sydney said.

"Gomez feels the same way," I told her. "He said he doesn't even want to go trick-or-treating!"

"If only Halloween wasn't all about candy," Sydney said.

I sighed. "I wish there was some way to help them."

"Maybe we could ask my dad," Sydney offered. "He loves Halloween and he doesn't even like candy. He's always playing pranks on the kids when they come to our house. Maybe he could help us make Halloween fun without the candy."

"It's worth a shot. What kind of pranks does he do?" I asked.

"He has a whole list," she said. "You should ask him."

"Awesome! I want to help Gomez prank Lucas, so that will solve one problem," I said.

"What about the candy problem?" Sydney asked.

"One problem at a time," I replied. "I promise to figure something out tonight."

I smiled confidently, but I had no idea how to solve the candy dilemma. I just knew I had to think of something or Halloween would be a bust.

CHAPTER 12

Little Brothers Will Ruin Your Life

As I walked through the front door after school, I almost tripped over Owen. He had just started crawling and was getting into everything. My parents had tried to set up gates around the house, but Owen was sneaky.

"Hey, little buddy!" I said. Sometimes having a baby brother could be a real pain. Other times it was really fun. Owen sat on the floor waving his arms like crazy and laughing. I couldn't help but laugh with him.

"There you are, silly boy!" my mom said as she walked down the hall toward us. She scooped up Owen and gave me a kiss.

"How was school today?" she asked me.

I followed her down the hall and told her about the new project we started in art. I saw Sidney's mom, Mrs. Fletcher, as we walked into the kitchen. I wasn't surprised to see her. She came over a lot.

"Hello, Sydney! What's this about a new art project?" Mrs. Fletcher asked. She's an artist, which I think is so cool! I want to be an artist one day, so I love talking with her. Her stories are amazing!

As I ate my snack, I told them about our new art project at school. "We each get our own canvas to paint on. Can you believe that?" I asked.

Canvas is the material that painters paint on. I felt like a real artist, having my own canvas.

"That is very exciting!" she said. "Having the right materials can take your art to a new level."

"I agree," I said. "If I'm going to be a great artist like you, I need to have the right materials. But now I have to check on my beautiful costume. See you later!"

"Bye, Sydney," Mrs. Fletcher said.

I ran up to my room. I wanted to try on my purple superhero princess costume one last time. Halloween was tomorrow, and that meant it was almost time to show off my costume at the school party!

I had been asking the other kids about their costumes. I felt pretty good about winning the best costume contest. I knew my costume was the most original.

I was just outside of my room when something caught my eye. A little figure was crawling out of the bathroom laughing. For just learning to crawl, Owen could sure get around and cause trouble.

When I looked into my room, I saw my bed. What I didn't see was my incredible superhero princess costume on top of my bed. I didn't want to panic right away.

I tried to figure out what had happened. Maybe mom had ironed it or took it downstairs to show Mrs. Fletcher.

Maybe I hung it in my closet and forgot. But the more I tried to calm down, the more panicked I got.

From that moment on, I felt like everything was in slow motion. I knew I had to go and see what Owen had done. I just knew it wasn't good. I slowly walked down the hall to the bathroom, and that's when I saw it.

"MOM!!!" I screamed.

Mom and Mrs. Fletcher found me in the bathroom, staring at the toilet. I was crying so hard I couldn't speak. All I could do was point to my costume, which was stuffed into the toilet.

"Oh, honey!" my mom said. "Owen must have gotten into your room! He is so sneaky now that he can crawl!"

My mom was holding Owen, and he was clapping and laughing. He thought this whole thing was funny.

A little while ago I thought my baby brother was cute. Now I never wanted to look at him again! Why couldn't I be an only child like Sidney?

"What am I going to do?" I cried. "The party is tomorrow, and I have no costume! My life is ruined!"

"Oh, Sydney," my mom said. "There's no need to be so dramatic."

"You just don't understand," I cried.

"I might have an idea," Mrs. Fletcher said. "We'll have to be creative, but it might be fun."

I didn't know what else to do, so I said, "Whatever." Just another thing to ruin Halloween.

Halloween, Gomez, and One Mean Older Brother

(again, but this time it ends better)

"Do you have everything?" Gomez asked me. We were heading to his house after school.

"Yep, I've got everything we need right here," I told him, patting my backpack.

After Sydney told me about her dad pulling pranks on Halloween, it made me think. I felt bad that Lucas always pulled pranks on Gomez. I decided to help Gomez get Lucas back.

Since my dad is gone, it's always fun to hang out with Mr. Greene. He is super funny! He told me all kinds of pranks I could do. He had a million of them!

Last year, he dressed like a scarecrow and sat very still on their front porch. Whenever a group of older kids came up to the house for candy, Mr. Greene would wait until they got very close. Then he would shout, "Boo!" He said every kid screamed, even Lucas.

So for the past few days, Gomez and I had been plotting our revenge on Lucas. We were finally ready. When we got to Gomez's house, it didn't take long to set up.

We were sitting at the kitchen table when Lucas and three of his friends came in after soccer practice.

As soon as Lucas walked in, he started teasing Gomez.

"Hey, shrimp! What are you babies doing?" he said, laughing at us. Lucas's friends laughed too, as if he was the funniest guy on earth.

"We're not doing anything, Lucas. Go away!" Gomez said.

But Lucas didn't go away. He came closer, and that's when he saw what was on the table. Apples, sticks, and sheets of caramel. His eyes got big.

"Are you making caramel apples?" he asked.

His friends came over to the table to look. Gomez pretended to hide some finished caramel apples behind his back, trying to stick to our plan.

"Go away, these aren't for you took us all afternoon to get these he said.

A big grin crossed Lucas's face. "Thanks for making them for us, little bro!" he said, slapping Gomez on the back.

"No!" Gomez yelled.

I tried hard not to laugh as Lucas picked up the finished balls of caramel on a stick and handed them to his friends.

"Eat up!" he told them.

Gomez and I watched as they all took huge bites out of the caramel apples. At first, they laughed as they ate. But within a few seconds, they began gagging and spitting out the food.

Gomez and I laughed and laughed.

"What is this?" Lucas yelled. He looked down at his hand.

"Caramel-covered onions," I said calmly.

"Happy Halloween!" we both said as we ran out of the kitchen laughing.

CHAPTER 14

And the Winner Is . . .

It was the day of the Halloween party, and I was in the girls' bathroom at school with Mrs. Fletcher. I stared at myself in the mirror and said, "Well, at least I know no one else will be dressed like me!"

"You look great!" Mrs. Fletcher said.

We started walking to my classroom. I could feel my heart pounding. I liked my costume. We'd worked really hard on it. I just hoped no one would laugh at me.

When we walked into Mr. Luther's room, I looked around. Everyone was in

their costumes. Sidney was dressed like
a magician, showing James a card trick.
James was dressed like a cat. Kara and
Alexa were both twirling around in
their matching princess costumes. Even
Mr. Luther was dressed up as a chef.

Gomez was dressed like a banana
and was making everyone laugh. He
kept running around the room shouting,
"B-A-N-A-N-A-S! Go, bananas! Go, go,
bananas!"

I laughed and started to relax.

"What have we here?" Mr. Luther asked
as he walked toward me.

Everyone in the room stopped talking.
They all looked at me.

"Um . . . I'm, um —" I mumbled.

"She's a painting," Sidney said. He and Gomez came over. "See? I helped with this part."

"And I helped with this part," Gomez said.

I stretched my arms out wide so everyone could see my costume. Mrs. Fletcher had taken a large piece of canvas, folded it over, and cut a hole in the top for my head. Then Harley, Gomez, Sidney, and I painted it. Even Owen helped.

On one side, we had painted our feet and walked across the canvas. Although I was mad at him for ruining my other costume, Owen's footprints looked the cutest.

On the other side, we did what Mrs. Fletcher called an "abstract" painting. I didn't know what "abstract" meant, but it was fun to paint! We all took turns splattering paint everywhere. I wore that side on my front.

"Very clever!" Mr. Luther said.

Before I knew it, the rest of the kids had gathered around and were checking out my costume.

The class party was so much fun! There were a bunch of different stations set up. I carved a pumpkin, won two games of Bingo, and learned a dance to the song "Monster Mash."

I was just about to play Pin the Face on the Jack-o'-Lantern when I heard Mr. Luther say, "Gather around, everyone! It's time to announce the costume awards."

This year, instead of one award, there were a few. Nick won for scariest costume. Gomez won for funniest costume.

And finally, Mr. Luther said, "And the award for most creative costume goes to ... Sydney Greene!"

I was so happy! It hadn't turned out like I expected, but this was the best Halloween ever.

And I already knew that it was just going to get better after school, when

Sidney and I finished our plan. Just as he had promised, he thought of the perfect solution to the candy problem.

CHAPTER 15

Best.
Halloween.
Ever.

After school, Sydney and I had to finish
the final part of our special Halloween
plan. It didn't take long to get everything
ready. And soon, we saw Harley and
Gomez walking down the street toward
Sydney's house.

"Here they come!" Sydney shouted as
she ran toward me.

I laughed a little because she looked
pretty funny trying to run in her painting
costume.

We took our places in the garage and waited. Inside the Greenes' garage, we had set up a haunted house. It was a lot of work, but it turned out so cool!

On one wall, there was a table full of gross stuff to touch. One bowl had a sign that read "Eyeballs" and was filled with peeled grapes. Another read "Mushed-Up Guts" and was full of cooked spaghetti.

My mom and Mrs. Greene were dressed as witches. They were going to stand at the table and try to spook the trick-or-treaters.

Owen was sitting in his playpen. It was filled with broken toys and dolls without heads and a bunch of purple fabric. The playpen had a sign on it that read Beware: This Baby Destroys Toys and Costumes! I thought it was hilarious!

Mr. Greene was dressed up like a mad scientist. He was standing at a table covered with bubbling pots. One pot was full of cooked hot dogs and had a sign that read "Fingers of Naughty Children."

On the outside of the garage, we'd set up a graveyard. Mr. Greene brought in dirt from the yard and made it look very real.

Gomez and I were going to hide in the bushes and jump out at people. I couldn't wait!

We also had a fog machine, flashing lights, scary music, and ghosts and bats that flew across the room on wires. It was awesome!

When Harley and Gomez finally walked into the garage, Sydney and I yelled, "Surprise!"

"What's going on?" Gomez asked.

"We decided that instead of going trick-or-treating, we're going to stay here and do a haunted house," I explained.

"But what about all the candy you'll miss?" Gomez asked.

I smiled and said, "Don't worry about that. We have treats inside. I know you and Harley can't have much sugar, so my mom set up a chocolate fountain for us to dip strawberries and graham crackers into. We even made caramel apples with sugar-free caramel."

Harley had a big smile on her face. That made Sydney smile too.

"Come on!" she said. "Our job is to direct kids in and out of the haunted house and to pass out candy. Let's get ready."

Gomez and I hid behind the bushes and covered ourselves with leaves.

"Are you sure you're okay with not going trick-or-treating?" Gomez asked me.

"I'm sure," I told him.

"This is the best Halloween ever," Gomez said.

And I agreed.

Sidney & Sydney

THOUGHTS ON . . .

GROWING UP

Sydney: I'm going to be a famous artist, a rock star, or a veterinarian.

Sidney: I'm going to play professional football in the fall, professional basketball in the winter, and professional baseball in the summer.

MR. LUTHER

Sydney: He may not smell like cherries like Mrs. Madden, but he has a nice smile.

Sidney: He's awesome! He has sports stuff all over the room and tells the funniest jokes!

RECESS

Sydney: Inside recess is better because we get to do crafts and draw.

Sidney: Outside is way better because we can play basketball and football. Inside is only okay if we can go in the gym.

CLOTHES

Sydney: It really depends on the weather. I usually like to wear skirts, but if it's too cold I love to wear a cute sweater and boots. Anything purple seems to work well for me.

Sidney: Who cares?

GALAXY CONQUEST

Sydney: I'm the best player. Sometimes I let him win.

Sidney: I'm the best player. Sometimes I let her win.

ABOUT THE AUTHOR

Raised in the Chicago suburb of Hoffman Estates, Michele Jakubowski has the teachers in her life to thank for her love of reading and writing. While writing has always been a passion for Michele, she believes it is the books she has read throughout the years, and the teachers who assigned them, that have made her the storyteller she is today. Michele lives in Powell, Ohio, with her husband, John, and their children, Jack and Mia.

ABOUT THE ILLUSTRATOR

Luisa Montalto followed a curved path to becoming an illustrator. She was first a dancer, then earned her doctorate degree in cinematography. She credits these experiences with giving her the energy and will to try harder. Finally, she went on to work with an independent comics magazine before becoming a professional illustrator in 2003.